Ghost Tales from the Oldest City

Suzy Cain

Illustrations by Dianne Jacoby

Pineapple Press, Inc.
Sarasota, Florida

Inquiries should be addressed to:
Pineapple Press, Inc.
P.O. Box 3889
Sarasota, Florida 34230

www.pineapplepress.com

Library of Congress Cataloging-in-Publication Data

Cain, Diana, 1956–
Ghost tales from the oldest city / Diana Cain and Dianne Jacoby. — First [edition].
    pages cm
 ISBN 978-1-56164-679-1 (pbk. : alk. paper)
1. Ghosts—Florida—Saint Augustine. 2. Haunted places—Florida—Saint Augustine. I. Title.
    BF1472.U6C34 2014
    133.109759'18—dc23

                                                    2013039403

First Edition
10 9 8 7 6 5 4 3 2 1

Printed in the United States

Table of Contents

Preface

St. Augustine is the oldest continuously occupied European city in the continental United States. Its diverse, rich, and fascinating history includes some fabulous stories about bizarre, haunted places and spaces and, of course, its legendary ghosts. These tales are celebrated in the many popular guided ghost tours, which is where I first heard the incredible stories that fill this book.

St. Augustine is a wonderful place to live and visit, with its miles of beautiful beaches, unparalleled hospitality, and quaint, cobbled streets. Its world-class historic sites include the Castillo de San Marcos National Monument, the St. Augustine Lighthouse, the Oldest House, the Oldest Wooden Schoolhouse, the Fountain of Youth. . . . The list goes on and on.

I hope you enjoy these strange ghost tales from the oldest city.

This book is dedicated to the residents of
St. Augustine, past and present.

Elizabeth

St. Augustine has many iconic landmarks, and the City Gate, built in 1808, remains my favorite. Its two strong, coquina columns guard the northern boundary of the historic district, the gateway to the heart of the colonial city. It once formed part of the Cubo defense line, a wall built around the perimeter of the city to provide protection for its residents.

But attacks from outsiders were not the only worry. Residents also had to be concerned about another pernicious invader: infectious disease. In 1821 a massive yellow fever epidemic struck St. Augustine. Many of its victims are buried in the Huguenot Cemetery—most of them in unmarked graves— located just outside the City Gate, where a lone, waiflike girl is often seen lingering. Locals call her Elizabeth and believe she was a victim of that tragic epidemic.

The Honorable Judge John B. Stickney

Just north of the City Gate lies the Huguenot Cemetery, also known as the Public Burying Ground. This half-acre plot was established in 1821, the same year Florida became a United States territory and people traveled in droves to this semitropical land to put down roots, improve their health, and make a fresh start. Unfortunately, another visitor arrived that year as well: yellow fever. Many victims of this epidemic were laid to rest in the Huguenot Cemetery.

It is said that the Huguenot Cemetery is home to many restless spirits, and one of the most interesting is Judge John B. Stickney. Judge Stickney was born in 1833 in Massachusetts. He, along with many others, moved to St. Augustine shortly after the Civil War ended. Rumormongers claimed that Judge Stickney was just another carpetbagger. However, he soon rose to a position of prominence and respect in his new home. Not only was he judge advocate but state's attorney and district attorney as well.

A widower, Judge Stickney did the best he could to make a life for himself and his children in St. Augustine. Often traveling on business, he was called away to Washington, D.C., in late October 1882. Despite feeling ill, he was determined to make the long and arduous journey north. He felt it was important business that simply could not wait.

The tiring trip took several days and included travel by rail, sea, and carriage. Shortly after he began his journey, he realized that he had made a grave mistake and should not have been traveling in such poor health. He pressed on, however, determined to get to Washington, where he almost collapsed and immediately took to his bed. His condition worsened and, five days later, Judge Stickney was found dead. The cause of death was listed as typhoid fever, and he had suffered a cerebral hemorrhage.

It was his wish to be buried in his adopted hometown of St. Augustine, so his body was shipped south. A memorial service was held in Trinity Episcopal Church, located on the southeast corner of King and St. George Streets. His popularity was evident by the many prominent politicians, businessmen, and dignitaries who attended the packed service on November 5, 1882. Afterwards, his body was taken to the Huguenot Cemetery for burial.

His children, now orphans, were adopted by Judge Long, a close friend and business associate of their father. They relocated with him to Washington, D.C., where they lived a contented life.

When Judge Long died in 1903, the children wanted their father's body moved to Washington to be reinterred next to the body of their adoptive father. So after twenty-one years of rest, Judge Stickney made his final journey north.

Gravedigger George Wells was responsible for exhuming the body and preparing it for shipment. He opened the grave in September 1903. As he began digging, a curious crowd gathered to watch. He worked efficiently and quickly, not paying much attention to the crowd. He removed the casket from the grave, opened it, and found the body to be in a good state of preservation. Satisfied, he was about to close the lid when he heard two intoxicated men singing at the top of their lungs. They lurched toward the cemetery, brandishing bottles of liquor. Seeing the crowd and wondering what all the fuss was about, they pushed through the throng up to Judge Stickney's casket. Before Mr. Wells could shut the lid, the men grabbed the judge's remains right out of the casket!

Confusion ensued. Mr. Wells chased the men off amidst lots of arguing and shouting. He returned the judge to his coffin and tidied up, but when he looked more closely, he saw that something was wrong. Unbelievably, all of Judge Stickney's gold teeth were missing! He spun around, but the two drunkards were long gone and several gold teeth richer. With nothing left to do, Mr. Wells quietly closed the lid and shipped the toothless, desecrated Judge Stickney north, hoping no one would notice.

Many people have seen the ghost of a well-dressed man roaming the cemetery, seemingly searching for something. Is it Judge Stickeny looking for his gold teeth? Or perhaps he's looking for the men who defiled his remains.

The Strange Case of the Bishop's Tomb

On the west side of Cordova Street sits the Tolomato Catholic Cemetery. This plot of land was once the site of a Native American village, and Christianized natives were the first to be buried there. Interments took place until 1884, when the cemetery was closed.

The first bishop of Florida, the Most Reverend Jean Pierre Augustine Mercellin Verot, died in June 1876. A special funeral Mass at the cathedral was planned, and mourners traveled from all over the Southeast to attend. To keep the body from deteriorating in the summer heat, ice had been ordered. The bishop's body was carefully placed in a hole in the ground lined with sawdust and ice. However, the ice quickly melted in the extreme heat, and church officials agreed they could wait no longer. The service would have to proceed even though some of the guests had not yet arrived. They lifted the bishop out of the sawdust-filled hole and placed his body in his special metal casket, which had a small glass window over the head and torso so mourners could view him during the service.

The service was well attended despite the stifling heat. The mourners crowded into the packed cathedral. Little did they know that something horrible was about to happen.

Natural bodily gases emanating from the less-than-perfectly preserved body had been building up inside the metal casket. The pressure and heat continued to build until the bishop's body actually exploded with amazing force! Glass shattered and sprayed, but more distressing was the horrible stench that immediately filled the space. Mourners ran from the cathedral, coughing and sputtering. Workers quickly cemented over the opening in the casket to stop the smell.

They needed to do something with the body—quickly. Someone suggested placing the bishop's body in the Varela Chapel at the rear of the Tolomato Cemetery. The Varela Chapel contained the remains of Felix Varela, a priest originally from

Cuba who had been buried there twenty-three years earlier.
Inside the small chapel, in the center of the floor, was a large
marble slab that covered Varela's remains. Workers carefully slid
the marble slab back, gathered up Varela's remains, and placed
them in an embroidered pillowcase. They lowered Verot's casket
into the vault and put the dainty pillowcase back inside as well.
Then they pushed the heavy marble slab back into place, and
the two prominent religious figures were left undisturbed for
the next thirty-five years.

Things ticked along fine until shortly after the turn of the century, when a group of Cuban citizens decided they wanted Felix Varela's remains in Cuba. Father Varela's ordination as a priest was nearing the centennial mark, and the citizens of Cuba wanted to honor people who had devoted their lives to democratic principles, including Father Varela. They contacted church officials in St. Augustine to ask about retrieving his remains.

A commission of Cuban dignitaries traveled north to St. Augustine. When the vault was opened, they took the delicate pillowcase containing the bones of Father Varela and headed back to Cuba. Strangely, there was no mention in the record of the second body in the vault.

Back in Cuba, monuments and statues were erected in Father Varela's honor, and his remains were placed in a special urn atop a large pedestal. But soon conflict arose. The author of a book published in the 1940s about the life of Father Varela claimed that the citizens of Cuba had been deceived. They had not been given the remains of their beloved Father Varela but those of Bishop Verot. Outraged, the Cubans hired scholars and scientists to examine the bones to determine to whom they really belonged.

After months of exhaustive research, the citizens of Cuba felt confident that the book was wrong and that they indeed had their man. Goodwill was restored, and the Cuban people were relieved that they had been honoring the remains of Father Varela all along.

Years later, in 1975, St. Augustine began preparing for the one hundredth anniversary of the death of Bishop Verot. The Diocese of St. Augustine planned a grand celebration, and, considering the confusion that had surrounded the remains, contacted military historian, academic, and author Dr. Michael Gannon to be a consultant. Dr. Gannon suggested that the only way to make sure the Cubans were right was to open Verot's casket and verify his remains. Dr. Gannon felt sure there would be two telltale signs: Bishop Verot's wooden dentures would still be intact, and his Pectoral Cross would be around his neck.

With the necessary tools in hand, workers lifted the casket out of the vault and began to dislodge the cement mixture so hastily applied one hundred years earlier. They put a chisel to the cement and began to *tap, tap, tap.* Suddenly, the chunk of cement popped off in one large piece. The stench was still overwhelming, and those present quickly fell over one another to get out of the tiny chapel. After a bit of debate, a brave photographer covered his face with a cloth and went back in to take some photos, which showed the bishop's wooden teeth and gold chain were intact.

The bishop's body was subsequently removed from the chapel and buried in the middle of the cemetery. A bust of the bishop sculpted by Ted Karam was installed over the grave in 1988. We can only hope he will now remain undisturbed for a very long time.

The Southern Wind Inn

Just south of the Tolomato Cemetery, at 18 Cordova Street, is a charming historic inn called The Southern Wind Inn. Built in 1916 as a private home in a development called the Anderson Tract, it became an apartment building during World War II. Now a lovely bed-and-breakfast, some of its owners have had multiple encounters with its ghost.

At first they weren't exactly sure what they were seeing. It *seemed* to be the figure of a woman. They saw her move through the hallway, caught a glimpse of her out on the balcony, or spied her loitering near the rear landing. But there was always a slight doubt in their minds that they had seen anything at all. No one else reported seeing anything strange.

Then guests slowly began mentioning things to them. One Friday evening two couples checked in for the weekend. One

couple was staying in the Veranda Room, the only room with a private entrance onto the balcony, which can be accessed from the hallway as well.

The other couple took a room at the far end of the hall, near the rear of the building. They put their luggage in their room and wandered down to the Veranda Room to discuss dinner plans with their friends. They knocked but didn't hear a reply or any noise in the room, so they went in. The husband saw a woman move from the bathroom through a small sitting area and out onto the balcony. He thought it strange and followed her to the balcony, but when he got out there she was gone! His wife had remained by the door, and there was no one in the hallway. Perplexed, they wandered back down the hall to their room and out onto the rear landing, only to see their friends in the parking lot, still unloading items from their car.

The staff also began to see the figure of a tall woman in a long white dress, often seated in a chair near the rear landing. Stranger yet, a woman who had once lived in the building when it was divided into apartments came by specifically to ask about the ghost. Interestingly, she too described a tall woman in white whom she frequently saw sitting in a chair near the rear landing.

The Ghost Bride

An elderly man who had spent his whole life in St. Augustine told this strange tale. He said he had experienced a good many things, but nothing stuck in his mind like the ghost he and his friends saw in the Tolomato Cemetery many years before.

When he was a young boy, he and his pals cooked up the ultimate pre-adolescent dare: spend the whole night in the Tolomato Cemetery. They formed a pact to sneak out of their homes on a Saturday night and meet near the cemetery entrance. At the stroke of midnight, they gathered, easily hopped over the wall, and crept in, being careful not to make a sound. They settled down near the back wall and took turns telling ghost stories. Suddenly they looked up and saw the figure of a woman dressed in white moving slowly toward them, weaving in and out among the headstones and trees.

Paralyzed with fear, they watched the figure come closer and closer. Just as she was almost close enough for them to reach out and touch her, they bolted and ran home as fast as they could without looking back.

The boys later described her as a "bride ghost." No one is quite sure who she is or why she remains in the Tolomato. Could she be the same spirit seen at The Southern Wind Inn just next door?

The Abbott Mansion

A beautiful late–nineteenth-century home at 14 Joiner Street that is now an inn is said to possess the spirit of its namesake, Lucy Abbott. She was the driving force behind the development of the Abbott Tract (which includes the inn) and was in fact Florida's first female real estate agent.

People who inhabited the home when it was an apartment building say they strongly felt her presence, and others who have stayed at the inn have seen her passing in the hallway. Many believe she is a malevolent ghost who doesn't want anyone in her house. Some have reported a force pushing them from behind when they are in a precarious spot—at the top of a staircase or near an open window, for instance. Others have heard unexplained knocking.

There have also been reports of a male ghost dressed in 1800s' sailors' garb. He doesn't seem to be associated with the female presence or to be an aggressive spirit.

The Opopanax Tree

Just after Florida became a United States territory, Colonel Joseph Smith arrived in St. Augustine in 1823 to be installed as the city's highest-ranking military official. It is said that he related this strange tale, which happened the first week he arrived.

As a senior official, Colonel Smith not only had his work commitments but also had to attend rounds of social functions. At a ball given in his honor, he met the most beautiful woman he had ever seen. The moment he saw her he was immediately and inconsolably infatuated. However, much to his dismay, he discovered that the woman was married. That evening he became acquainted with her and her husband and despite (or maybe because of) his feelings, they hit it off and became fast friends. When the evening came to a close, they looked forward to the next time they would meet, but, alas, it was not meant to be.

In the wee hours of the next morning, the woman became violently ill. The doctor was called in, but no one seemed able to do a thing for her. Within a week, she was pronounced dead.

Distraught, her husband turned to his newfound friend, Colonel Smith, and invited him to walk by his side in the funeral procession. Of course, the colonel agreed. It was a family custom to carry the deceased to the gravesite seated in a chair. How odd it must have been to see this beautiful woman floating along the road above the pallbearers in an ornate chair, mourners following close behind. With every bump in the road, her head lolled back and forth.

As the mourners entered the Tolomato Cemetery, they passed under the thorny branches of the opopanax tree. One of its thin branches pierced her temple, and a small trickle of blood slid down the side of her face. Colonel Smith, who had not taken his eyes off her the entire time, shouted that she was not dead, that he had seen her eyes blink. She was alive!

The husband and other mourners were embarrassed by Smith's sudden outburst and, despite his insistence, carried on with the burial. He continued to plead with them; they finally relented and carried her back to her home. They watched and waited and in a few minutes were shocked to see her eyelids flutter. Had it not been for Colonel Smith, the beautiful woman would have been buried alive.

She thrived for another six years when she died "again." Once more mourners carried her body to the cemetery in the ornate chair. This time, however, as they approached the opopanax tree, the procession abruptly stopped when her husband blurted out, "Whatever you do, don't take her too close to the opopanax tree!"

The Nun and
the Soldier

The Peso de Burgo-Pellicer House stands at 49 St. George Street. A reconstruction of a Minorcan duplex, it is an important part of St. Augustine's historic district. The building that had previously occupied the site was the Paffe family business, a combination stationery-toy store and print shop. The matron of the Paffe family lived with her grandson in an apartment above the shop.

The grandmother was a strong woman, but her health had been declining. She eventually required full-time care, and her grandson hired a nurse named Maggie Hunter to help him care for her overnight.

A huge storm was brewing when Maggie arrived on her first day of work. The wind howled and continued to get stronger as the evening progressed. Maggie met with the grandson in his room at the opposite end of the hall from his grandmother's room. They discussed the care she would need, and he told Maggie that if she needed him in the middle of the night, it was no problem to wake him.

Maggie thanked the grandson and went down to the kitchen to get the old woman a glass of milk. As she approached the grandmother's room, she was startled to see the figure of a nun kneeling by the bed, praying.

She quietly turned around, thinking the nun had arrived while she was getting the milk, and asked the grandson about it. He was unconcerned and said, "Oh, I'm glad the nun is here tonight. Grandmother must have been frightened by the storm."

Reassured, Maggie went back to the grandmother's room, only to find that the nun had disappeared. She did not know what to make of it but didn't want to concern the grandson again and comfortably settled into the chair next to the grandmother's bed.

The next few weeks were peaceful and uneventful. Then one night, Maggie went to the kitchen to prepare of bowl of soup for the elderly woman. On her way back to the room, soup in hand, she encountered an eighteenth-century Spanish solider in full uniform, marching down the hall away from the grandmother's room and right toward her. She dropped the bowl and ran to the grandson's room. When she told him what she had seen, he practically knocked her over as he ran down the hall to his grandmother.

Maggie raced down the hall after him and found him by his grandmother's bed, crying and muttering something about the nun and repeating, "Why did the soldier have to come? Why?" When he had calmed down, he explained to Maggie that the nun appeared when his grandmother was frightened and gave her comfort. But his grandmother had always told him, "When it is my time to go, a soldier will come and take me away."

Sure enough, his grandmother passed away that night, and no one ever saw the ghost of the soldier or nun again.

Castillo de San Marcos

Undoubtedly, St. Augustine's most impressive landmark is the Castillo de San Marcos, now part of the National Park Service. Construction of this impressive fortress began in 1672 and took 23 years to complete. It is made of coquina, a native shell rock that was quarried on Anastasia Island, the barrier island that lies just over the Bridge of Lions. The Castillo is the oldest masonry fortress in the United States, a massive structure symbolizing centuries of Spanish control in the New World.

There are many stories connected to the Castillo, and one that remains intriguing is the story of the Seminole leader Osceola. During the Second Seminole War, Osceola had evaded capture by the U.S. military but was finally tricked, under the pretense of a white flag, and taken prisoner just south of St. Augustine. He was transported to the Castillo and held there along with 200 other Seminoles.

The conditions were harsh. The fortress was damp, dark, and moldy. Osceola was a strong man, but being imprisoned broke his spirit. When he became terribly ill, local doctor Dr. Frederick Weedon came to treat the ailing leader. Osceola was diagnosed with malaria and transferred to Fort Moultrie, South Carolina, where he died soon after his arrival.

During the brief time Dr. Weedon cared for Osceola in St. Augustine, he became fascinated with him. He admired his courage, strength of character, and intelligence and found him to be a remarkable man on many levels. Because of his strong feelings for Osceola, he wanted to pay his final respects and decided to make the long journey to Fort Moultrie to attend his funeral service.

No one knows the real reason—perhaps it was his infatuation and fascination with Osceola—but Dr. Weedon decided he wanted Osceola's head. His intention was to preserve it for posterity via mummification. At some point he was alone with the body. With a scalpel, he carefully severed the head from the body, but he didn't take the head yet. Before anyone returned, he carefully wrapped the scarf Osceola typically wore back around the warrior's neck to hide his handiwork.

Weedon wasn't sure if he would have another chance to be alone with the body to grab the head, but at the gravesite he had just that chance. When no one was looking, he quickly took the head, placed it in a bag, and carried it back to St. Augustine. Amazingly, no one discovered that Osceola's head was missing, and he was buried without it.

Back in St. Augustine, Dr. Weedon worked diligently to preserve the head. He also made a death mask from it. Legend has it that when his children misbehaved, he would place the mummified head on their bedpost, staring down at them as they tried to sleep. We can be fairly certain they didn't misbehave very often.

Eventually, Dr. Weedon gave the mummified head to his son-in-law, who in turn gave it to a New York physician, who placed it on exhibit at the Surgical and Pathological Museum. Unfortunately, the museum was destroyed by a fire in 1866 and, along with it, presumably, Osceola's head, though this was never officially verified.

Another intriguing Castillo story began when Sergeant Tuttle and his men were moving a large cannon on the gun deck in 1838. As they pushed the heavy cannon, the gun deck suddenly gave way, plunging the cannon to the level below. They ran down to recover it and, to their surprise, discovered a wall that must have sealed up an empty space. They speculated that there must be a secret room beyond the wall and excitedly began chipping away at it. Hoping to find not only the cannon but some kind of treasure, they were disappointed to discover a small room with a low ceiling that had once been used to store gunpowder.

Although the secret room turned out to be rather mundane, they did discover bones among the ashes and leftover gunpowder. Stories started circulating about the secret dungeon room. As time went by, the stories became more exaggerated, particularly at the turn of the twentieth century, when tour guides at the fort discovered that their tips were proportional to the fantastic tales they told. One story even claimed that a former governor of St. Augustine found his wife with her lover and, enraged, sealed them in the dungeon room to meet their death.

None of these stories have been substantiated, and there isn't an actual dungeon in the Castillo. However, some visitors say they feel an eerie coldness when they visit the small gunpowder room in the northeast corner.

A Cry in the Night

Built in 1910, a large family home stands adjacent to a public parking lot in Tocques Place. The family who built the home lived there until 1960. They had a daughter who became pregnant when she was just a teenager. Her mother decided it would be prudent to keep the pregnancy a secret, so she and her daughter stayed in their house throughout most of the pregnancy. They decided that the mother would claim the baby was hers and raise the child along with the daughter.

A woman who worked for the family served as midwife and delivered a healthy son. Even after the birth, the mother and daughter stayed close to home to avoid confrontation and unwelcome questions. The boy was a happy baby but, sadly, he contracted encephalitis and died when he was two. The family was heartbroken. Overwhelmed by sadness, they couldn't bear to stay in the house, which became a rental property.

To save money by sharing expenses, two couples agreed to rent the house. Both couples had children, and both husbands worked away from home for extended periods. The wives cared for the children. The women slept in the bedrooms downstairs while all of the children occupied the upstairs rooms.

One night, one of the older boys came downstairs and woke his mother, saying that one of the younger boys was crying and wouldn't stop. The mother listened for some time, heard nothing, and sent the boy back to bed. It wasn't long before he came back down, saying it was still going on. Would she come up and check?

She went upstairs only to discover all of the children sound asleep in their beds. She reassured the child that it was only a dream and sent him back to bed again, telling him to come get her immediately if he heard anything else.

A short while later, he was down in her room again. He said that it was not the younger boy at all but a small boy whom he had never seen before. He told her that the boy was crying at the top of the stairs and wouldn't stop. The mother leaped from her bed and ran to the bottom of the stairs, but when she got there the boy had vanished. Of course, the crying specter is believed to be the ghost of the little boy who died in the house.

Years later, workers remodeling the house discovered a small closet under the stairs that had been sealed up. When it was opened, a child's ball bounced out, and inside sat a brand-new tricycle waiting for the baby boy to become old enough to use it.

The Woman with
the Suitcase

Along the bayfront at 22 Avenida Menedez stands a beautiful house that was built in 1915 by John D. Puller, a prominent local banker. Now a private home, it was once a historic inn called the Casa de la Paz. The couple who ran the inn did extensive renovations when they took over ownership and held an open house for invited guests once the work was completed.

That night, guests and friends enjoyed drinks and canapés before the owner positioned himself in the middle of the staircase to address the crowd below. As he spoke, he noticed that a woman in the crowd was distracted and kept looking beyond him to the top of the stairs. Somewhat annoyed, he finished his speech and invited the guests to enjoy more food and drink and have a look around. The woman who had been so distracted approached him and apologized, explaining that she had seen the figure of a woman in a long narrow skirt, a traveling jacket, and a wide-brimmed hat suddenly appear at the top of the stairs. She was carrying a small suitcase and lingered for a moment as if she wanted to come down but couldn't because the way was blocked by the owner. The next minute she was gone. Many guests who subsequently stayed at the Casa de la Paz saw her frequently.

The ghost at the top of the stairs is a woman who once stayed in the lovely home with a group of others while visiting friends and family in town. She became ill and, after a protracted illness, died in the house. Her traveling companions reluctantly left, and her spirit remained behind.

When the house was divided into apartments, just before it became an inn, some residents reported hearing a soft knocking on the door and then a small voice asking, "Is it time to leave yet? Is it time to leave?" Others heard a door slam shut and then saw the ghost walking down the hall with her bag. She was usually seen at the top of the stairs, standing forlornly in her traveling clothes, bags packed and ever hopeful to depart.

Strange Little Demons

On Hypolita Street, between Charlotte and St. George Streets, stands a lovely old house that in one of its many incarnations was a charming tearoom. A small apartment on the top floor came furnished with the usual items—sofa, tables, beds, etc.— as well as a number of primitive African artifacts including wooden masks, statues, and sculptures.

A brother and sister who once rented the apartment told this unusual story. The siblings ran a burgeoning business in town and also operated a gift shop on the west coast of Florida. They often traveled back and forth across the state between their businesses. One weekend they had just such a trip scheduled. Their plan was to head out early Saturday morning. On Friday night, they had dinner just down the road at the White Lion Tavern and returned home to turn in early for a good night's sleep.

The sister slept in the tiny bedroom, and the brother slept on the sofa bed in the living room. Just as they were both ready to drop off, they sensed something moving quickly across the floor. The brother jumped up, thinking it was a mouse or a rat, and flicked on the lights. He asked his sister if she had seen what it was, but she said she couldn't be sure. They searched the apartment but found nothing out of the ordinary.

Thinking it was their imagination, they chalked it up to being tired and went back to bed. A moment later, it happened again. They both leaped from their beds and to their astonishment saw two diminutive, humanlike figures darting across the floor. In an instant they were gone.

Frightened and bewildered, the sister said her immediate instinct was to cut out paper crosses and tape them to all of the African artifacts. She quickly finished her task and insisted that they leave that night, even if they had to drive through the night or get a hotel along the way. Her brother agreed. Neither wanted to stay in the apartment another minute.

They threw some clothes into their bags, locked the door, and headed out, driving through the night. Late that Sunday night when they arrived back home, they tentatively opened the apartment door, wondering what they might find. Everything was as they had left it—except that every one of the paper crosses had been burned to ashes. Nothing remained but tiny bits of charred paper, ashes, and the tape that had held the crosses to the artifacts. No one else had a key to the apartment, and the landlord lived out of town.

Shaken and even more frightened, the siblings spoke to some friends about the incident. One of the friends suggested that the artifacts might have special religious significance and weren't meant for secular or decorative purposes. He proposed that demons or spirits had escaped from the masks in anger and burned the paper crosses on their way out.

This possibility didn't sit well with the siblings, and they soon moved out. The artifacts were removed as well. It is not known what became of them, but we can hope the tiny demons are at peace.

The Events

A story that even the most emphatic non-believer will find convincing was recounted by a former mayor of St. Augustine, Kenny Beeson. He says the "events," as he liked to call them, began quite a few years ago with an unusual odor.

Mr. Beeson owned Kixies Men's Shop, which was located at 138 St. George Street. He enjoyed his work and the social interaction that a retail establishment allowed. During his time there, he experienced a number of strange occurrences: door knobs turning by themselves, objects being moved when no one was there, and the unusual odor, which he said was sweet and cloying. It would mysteriously arrive with no apparent source and vanish just as abruptly. The most frightening aspect was that no one else seemed to smell it. Additionally, it would occur not only in the shop but at home and in public places, inside and outside.

Mr. Beeson often worked in the evenings in his shop when it was quiet and he could get a lot done. The television was usually on to keep him company. One particular night, coincidently, he was watching a program about supernatural experiences. Shortly after dinner, a friend dropped by to visit. Mr. Beeson continued sewing, talking as he worked.

Suddenly, the stockroom door slowly opened and the now-familiar smell wafted out. Mr. Beeson smelled it right away but didn't say anything. Would his friend smell it too? Yes, he did. His friend jokingly remarked that Mr. Beeson was wearing some awfully strong cologne.

Though Mr. Beeson was relieved that someone else had finally noticed the odor, both men were shocked that the stockroom door had opened by itself. They peered into the stockroom but saw nothing. For a few moments they sat in silence. Mr. Beeson happened to be staring at the bathroom door when he noticed the knob slowly turning. Then . . . *boom!* The door burst open. Mr. Beeson's friend suggested that they get the heck out of there.

Mr. Beeson readily agreed but wanted to do something first. He had just purchased a new tape recorder and thought he would set it up to see if he could capture anything on tape. His friend waited anxiously by the back door while Mr. Beeson set the recorder to play. As the men were leaving and the friend stepped over the threshold, Mr. Beeson saw the reflection of a man's face on his friend's back. It was there for a few seconds and then disappeared. Given how upset his friend was, Mr. Beeson never mentioned the reflection.

The next morning, Mr. Beeson arrived at the shop early, eager to play the tape back to see if it had recorded anything unusual. The first noise he heard sounded like soldiers marching in the street. Then he heard what sounded like animals rummaging around in the shop. These noises lasted quite some time and were punctuated by high-pitched squeals, "like a rodent's." He also heard the sound of a ship's bell tolling.

Not long after Mr. Beeson recorded the eerie sounds, his friend who had visited died of a heart attack. He had had no history of heart trouble, and his death was a shock to everyone.

At the funeral service, Mr. Beeson smelled the familiar sweet odor. Then he noticed that the man he had seen reflected on his friend's back in his shop was standing right in front of him! It was his friend's brother. He had never met him before, but he was sure this was the man he had seen in the reflection. If that was not strange enough, it was only a short time later that his friend's brother died as well.

Much to Mr. Beeson's dismay, the odd "events" continued at 138 St. George Street. He decided to install an alarm system to see if it would help, but it didn't. One day the alarm failed completely. Mr. Beeson climbed into the crawl space to inspect it, only to find that the wires had been cut. At that point, he decided to try another tack.

He spoke to the monsignor at the cathedral, explaining everything that had taken place in the shop. The monsignor listened intently and told Mr. Beeson he thought an exorcism was needed. It seemed to have worked, as the unusual "events" ceased to occur. Mr. Beeson did continue to smell the distinct sweet odor from time to time, though not as frequently. He later learned that sweet odors that seem to come from nowhere are associated with death. You may encounter a cloying smell just prior to someone's death or in a location where someone has died.

In an unusual postscript, the same psychics who described the de Mesa Sanchez House (later in the book) as a "bubble of evil" wanted to see the rear of the shop at 138 St. George Street. After spending some time at the site, they said there was a "portal" by the rear door through which spirits could pass into our dimension. They felt this might explain the reflection that Mr. Beeson saw on his friend's back. They also felt, however, that the paranormal activity in the shop was far from over, despite the monsignor's exorcism.

Hotel Ponce de Leon

The Hotel Ponce de Leon opened in 1888 to enormous success. An impressive architectural achievement, it was the first poured-concrete building of its size in the United States, and it became a haven for wealthy Northerners: a place to spend the winter months in a luxurious setting in a semitropical clime. The hotel boasted 450 rooms, a private dining hall with Tiffany stained glass windows, reading rooms, and private parlors, all lavishly appointed and meticulously designed.

Henry Flagler, one of the founders of the Standard Oil Company, had a dream: to open Florida to tourism. With his Hotel Ponce de Leon, his dream had begun to take root. However, his vision of transforming St. Augustine into the Newport of the South was never truly achieved. Visitors in search of more consistent balmy weather opted to travel farther south. So Mr. Flagler went south as well. He built the Florida East Coast Railroad all the way to Key West, and, along the way, he built more magnificent hotels.

Henry died in 1913 at Whitehall, his luxurious home in Palm Beach, but his desire was to be buried in his beloved St. Augustine. His body was transported by his private rail coach northward, then carried to the Hotel Ponce de Leon by carriage. Hundreds of mourners lined the streets to get a glimpse of his coffin. His body lay in state in the rotunda of the hotel, and hundreds more came to pay their final respects to the founder of Florida tourism.

It was a close, humid, drizzly day with absolutely no wind. The massive doors to the rotunda were propped wide open, but in the midst of the viewing, the huge doors slammed shut on their own. It is said that Henry's spirit circled the rotunda until it grazed the floor, leaving an impression of his face on one of the small marble tiles. The doors were reopened and his spirit was free to leave. Visitors can still look for his image on the floor today.

The Hotel Ponce de Leon became Flagler College in 1968. First established as a women's college, it soon became a co-educational institution offering four-year liberal arts degrees. What were once grand hotel rooms from a bygone era are now dormitories, and the gorgeous dining room is now the students' dining hall.

Over the years, many students have reported odd experiences in the buildings that now comprise Flagler College. Some have seen ghosts in their rooms or in the hallways. Others have been awakened from a sound sleep to discover the specter of Henry Flagler himself standing by their beds.

One student would yell "Hi, Henry" as he passed the tile with the miniature face imprinted on it. One evening he was in his dorm room alone, studying. His roommate was at work and would not return until much later. Suddenly, he heard a small creaking noise. He looked up to see that the door to his room had opened just a crack. Jokingly, he called out "Come on in, Henry!" With that, the door opened farther and then all the way, but no one was at the door. He went out into the hall, only to find it empty. Frightened, he returned to his room, shut the windows, locked the door, and went to his roommate's workplace. He had no desire to go back to the room alone, so he waited for his roommate to finish work. When they got back to the room, unlocked the door, and went in, all the windows were wide open.

Quite an odd story from another student involves miniature people similar to those in the Strange Little Demons story. One night she was in her dorm room, reading in bed and occasionally dozing. Almost asleep with her eyes closed, she suddenly felt pressure on her chest. She opened her eyes and was startled to see two very small people staring at her. Wondering if she was dreaming, she closed her eyes and pulled the covers over her head. Slowly, she lowered the sheet only to find they were still there. She bolted from the room, leaving the door wide open. She ran down the hall to a friend's room, and when they returned the door was locked. When they retrieved a spare key and opened the door, there was no trace of the diminutive figures.

Perhaps the most frequently seen ghost haunting the former Hotel Ponce de Leon is that of Ida Alice, Henry's second wife. She had been the nurse for his first wife, who died after a prolonged illness. It wasn't long after his first wife's death that Henry married Ida Alice, and some people felt it was his undoing. Ida Alice loved the lifestyle Henry's wealth afforded, and the couple spent a good deal of time at the hotel.

Not long into the marriage, Ida Alice became mentally ill and violent. She would lock herself in one of the hotel's rooms with a Ouija board and "listen" to what it told her. She became convinced that the czar of Russia wanted to marry her and even plotted to kill Henry so she could become the czarina. Sadly, her doctors felt that she was dangerous and would never recover so she was institutionalized for the rest of her life. Her ghost is often seen on the upper floors of the former hotel, dressed in a long gown and fine jewels, as was her custom in life.

The Red Blouse

A couple who lived in an apartment along St. George Street near the cathedral reported this peculiar story that all started with a gift from one of the sisters of St. Joseph's Convent.

The couple owned a restaurant on Aviles Street, just up the road from the convent. They would often see the sister walking along Aviles Street early in the morning on her way to and from the cathedral. They always exchanged pleasant greetings and eventually became better acquainted. One day the sister gave the wife a gift, a lovely red blouse. The woman was quite touched by the kindness, but she never wore red. She carefully put the blouse on a hanger and put it in the back of her closet.

A few weeks later, the couple was invited to a dinner party. The wife came home from work and went into the bedroom to change, only to discover the red blouse on the bed, laid out for her to wear. She asked her husband if he had put it there, but he said he hadn't and had no idea how the blouse got there. She laughed and shook her head, wondering if her husband was playing a trick on her. She returned the red blouse to the rear of the closet.

A week later, she came home to find a book she had already read and put away lying open on her pillow. It almost seemed to be an invitation to pick the book up and read it. She asked her husband if he knew why it was there, but again he said he knew nothing about it. Now they were both perplexed but thought there must be a logical explanation for these strange events.

Several days later, their dog began to act strangely. He growled at things that weren't there and cowered for no reason. Then a very odd thing happened. When they went to work in the morning, the couple would leave their dog in their second-floor apartment. One evening they came home to find the dog outside in courtyard. They were certain he couldn't have jumped two stories to the ground, but how did he get there?

Other unexplained things happened as well. Items were moved when no one was home. The couple developed a general feeling of unease and became so concerned they spoke to a friend about it. The friend suggested they have a psychic visit the apartment. Though skeptical, they figured they had nothing to lose.

As the psychic was climbing the stairs, she suddenly froze. At her heels, the couple's dog began to growl loudly. His fur was standing on end, and his ears were pinned back against his head. An intense coldness enveloped them. The psychic carefully and slowly moved into the living room and said she was picking up a very strong presence in the apartment. She said it was a man named Henry. She thought she might be able to convince Henry to leave, but when she sat down to try to communicate with him, a loud noise outside interrupted her attempt.

The couple was distraught. Unsettling events continued to occur. In fact, they found out that their ghost wasn't confined to their apartment. One morning as they enjoyed coffee and doughnuts with their neighbor across the hall, she announced that she reckoned she had a ghost. One night when she was home alone, washing the dishes, she felt a sharp slap on her backside. She joked that if she did have a ghost, it was definitely a man and a fresh one at that!

The couple were at their wits' end. Through the grapevine, they heard about the ghosts in Mr. Beeson's shop just down the street and his successful solution. They too contacted the church and asked a representative to come to the apartment. They claim this did the trick: no more weird experiences, no more visitations, and their dog was back to normal. Henry seems to have vanished into thin air.

Interestingly, the couple discovered that a seafaring man named Henry Barnes had lived at their address some years back when he came ashore. Perhaps this Henry is only temporarily out to sea.

The Murder of Lieutenant Delaney

On the night of November 20, 1785, during the Second Spanish Period, a brutal attack took place at the corner of Treasury and Charlotte Streets. The crime remains unsolved to this day.

The victim was Lieutenant Guillermo Delaney, a young officer in the Spanish army who, like many men, had been infatuated with the beautiful and seductive Catalina Morain. Catalina, a seamstress, was occasionally hired to mend the soldiers' uniforms, but there was speculation that she provided more personal services as well.

On the night of the attack, Lt. Delaney was on his way to see the lovely Catalina. Walking along the cobbled street alone that dark, cool night, anticipating the time he would spend alone with Catalina, he was suddenly attacked by two people in hooded cloaks. They beat and stabbed him and left him for dead in a pool of blood in the narrow street.

Bleeding profusely and in great pain, Lt. Delaney dragged himself the rest of the way to Catalina's home. She took him in, tended to his wounds, and nursed him back to reasonable health. A few months later, however, Lt. Delaney died. Now what had been an assault was upgraded to murder.

The governor ordered the unprovoked murder investigated. Weeks dragged into months as suspects were called and questioned, but nothing was proven and no one was charged.

Many people who have been on various guided ghost tours say they felt a bizarre coldness when they arrived at the corner of Treasury and Charlotte Streets. A sudden gust of wind perhaps? Or could it be the dark, sad shadow of Lt. Guillermo Delaney?

Casablanca Inn

During the 1920s and early 1930s, rumrunners traveled up and down the East Coast, passing through St. Augustine in boats laden with bootleg liquor. They sailed up from the Caribbean with their cases of rum and would often arrive in St. Augustine's harbor just after dusk.

At the time, the opulent Casablanca Inn at 24 Avenida Menendez was a boardinghouse run by an intrepid widow who had a lucrative business deal with the bootleggers. She allowed them to operate a small "shop" in the building—for a decent cut of their profits, of course—and it wasn't long before guests and locals knew where they could obtain the best hooch in town. The smugglers would arrive with their goods, stay for a few days, make their money, and then cruise farther north to their next setup.

Despite Prohibition—or because of it really—her business was absolutely booming, but it wasn't long before the police got wind of the operation and tried to shut her down. Eventually, federal officers arrived in town and questioned everyone, including the widow. They even tried to bribe her in exchange for information, but she knew she had a good thing going and kept her mouth shut. She was also smart enough to realize that they would be back again in an attempt to arrest her and the bootleggers, so she quickly worked out a plan.

She knew the bootleggers' schedule intimately and told them that when the government boys were in town, she would stand on the widow's walk atop the boardinghouse and wave a lantern back and forth to warn them. That way they could bypass St. Augustine and sail to their next destination, avoiding certain capture.

Guests staying on the upper floors of the inn adjacent to the Casablanca have noticed a moving light shining through their windows at dusk. Shrimpers and fishing crews say they often still see a single light swinging back and forth on top of the Casablanca, a light that strangely disappears once they safely pass through the inlet.

Ann O'Malley's Pub

Just west of the City Gate, at 23 Orange Street, stands Ann O'Malley's, a charming, friendly pub where you can get a superb sandwich and an ice-cold pint. Former owners, a husband and wife, told this strange tale.

It was a slow night with few customers. By the end of the night, only a close friend was sitting at the bar, enjoying a cold brew. The husband wasn't feeling well and decided he would go home early. His wife offered to stay behind and close up and asked him to call when he got home. He gave her a kiss, went out through the back door, and got into his car.

The wife grabbed a rag and began wiping down the tables when she heard her husband call her name. She went back to the kitchen to see what he wanted, but he wasn't there. She looked everywhere, even outside. He was nowhere to be found, and his car was gone. But she was sure she had heard him distinctly and loudly call her name only moments before.

She went back to the bar and questioned her friend. Had *he* heard her husband call her name? Yes, he was absolutely sure he had heard someone call her name. The next moment, the phone rang, startling her. It was her husband, saying he was home. He had arrived more than ten minutes earlier.

Catalina's Garden

Along the bayfront, at 46 Avenida Menendez, stands a seafood restaurant with a beautiful, walled courtyard. The building, originally a house built in 1750, has gone through a number of incarnations, among them a restaurant called Catalina's Garden, named for one of the children of the original owners.

In 1763 the British took possession of Florida. Those loyal to the Spanish crown departed for Cuba, including Catalina and her family. She spent her formative years in Cuba and eventually married there. But when Spanish rule returned to Florida in 1783, she became homesick and wanted to return to St. Augustine and the home where she was born. She petitioned the government and delightedly regained possession of her former bayfront home.

After Catalina's death, the house changed hands several times. Sadly, in 1887 a massive fire swept along St. Augustine's

bayfront, destroying many historic buildings, including the one that had been Catalina's home. Fortunately, it was rebuilt to mirror the original structure.

In recent years, the building has been home to a variety of restaurants, and many people have reported seeing two separate ghosts in the building. One of the apparitions, seen only downstairs, is a stoic-looking man dressed in black, period clothing and an old-fashioned black hat. A female diner was the first to notice him. He stood quietly next to the fireplace, standing absolutely still and staring directly at her, which she found quite unnerving. He seemed completely oblivious to what was going on around him. After a few minutes, she got up to tell the management about him. When they came to ask him to leave, he had vanished without a trace.

Another woman saw the man in black after she had returned downstairs from the women's restroom. As she walked into the main dining room, she saw him standing near the large wine case. She thought it was odd to see someone dressed in such authentic, vintage clothing, and she couldn't take her eyes off him. Then, right before her eyes, he passed through the wine case and was gone.

A second ghost appears only upstairs. A staff member was busy folding napkins at the workstation next to the women's restroom when he heard a bloodcurdling scream. A female patron flung open the door of the restroom and bolted from the bathroom with her slacks down around her knees, pulling them up as she ran all the way down the stairs. She was disoriented and was shouting, "I had to get out. There was something horrible in there. I didn't see anything. I just felt some kind of awful presence. It was like someone was staring directly at me."

Several of the restaurant's wait staff have described seeing the figure of a woman dressed in white on the second floor. Some employees have seen her reflection in a mirror, but when they turn around she's gone. While no one can definitively identify the ghost, most people believe it's Catalina's spirit.

Aside from the massive fire that destroyed the original home, fire seems to cause problems in this haunted place. On a number of occasions, the fireplace has spontaneously burst into flames when no one has been near it. A staff member once noticed a thick plume of smoke rising from a laundry hamper. He removed all of the towels and linen napkins and dug down to the bottom. There was nothing there, however, that would have caused a fire.

The ghosts of 46 Avineda Menendez continue to come and go. Perhaps someday their true identities will be revealed.

Casa de Horruytiner

At 214 St. George Street, south of the Plaza de la Constitution, is a magnificent home that has been associated with spirits for years. The house dates back to the First Spanish Period and was the residence of two governors, both from the Horruytiner family.

The owners who lived in the house in the late 1990s spoke of many peculiar events. They were excited and intrigued, especially when things began happening the moment they moved in. Standing in the foyer, the wife proclaimed, "You know, if there are spirits here, I wish they would make themselves known." With that, the living room, hallway, and stairwell lights turned on spontaneously. The husband joked, "If I had known this house was haunted, we would have paid *more* money for it!"

They loved living in the home and were charmed by one of the earlier stories that involved Brigita Gomez, who lived in the home with her husband sometime after 1783. Brigita was well known for her green thumb and spent many hours tending the gorgeous plants and delicate flowers that grew in a lovely walled garden on the south side of the house.

One day while working in the garden, she felt a strong presence. She turned and saw the figures of two women gliding slowly toward her. For some reason, she wasn't afraid and wanted to communicate with them. As they got closer, they did indeed speak to her. One woman claimed to be Maria Ruiz Horruytiner, the wife of one of the former governors. The other introduced herself as Antonia de Pueyo. Brigita was absolutely fascinated and excitedly asked them many questions about the past. They spoke for a long time and when the spirits departed, Brigita presented them with a bouquet of her celebrated yellow roses.

Exhilarated and breathless, she ran into the house to tell her husband what had happened. Not sharing her enthusiasm for the paranormal, he made light of the situation and asked if she had perhaps been in the sun too long.

The next morning, Brigita was still reeling from the experience, but her husband did not want to discuss it. He did not believe in ghosts and did not want to encourage her folly. There would be no more talk of ghosts. He dressed and got ready to go to work. As he was leaving by the front door, he almost tripped over the bouquet of Brigita's yellow roses lying on the threshold. All Brigita could do was smile.

Happily, all of the resident ghosts appear to be benevolent, including the ghost of a Spanish soldier who seems to be guarding the house. Many residents have seen him over the years and have said they had a good feeling about him. Having the ghost of a soldier in your home is thought to be a good sign as it is a symbol of protection and strength.

Not surprisingly, one of the home's most loved apparitions is that of a cheeky calico cat. The husband was home in his office one day when a stray cat jumped up on his desk. He and his wife had their own cats, but he had never seen this one before. He reached out to pat its head, and his hand passed right through the cat's body. He chuckled and called it his "Spanish cat."

Weeks later, his young grandson was visiting and went into the front room to look for something. He saw the calico cat

run out of the room and quickly scurry up the stairs. He knew that his grandparents didn't allow their cats to go into the front room and asked his grandfather, "Grandpa, did you get a new calico cat?" The grandfather replied, "No, that's just my Spanish cat. Don't worry about her. She can go into any room she likes."

One evening the grandson was sitting in the living room with his grandmother, reading a book. They were suddenly interrupted by the vision of a man in eighteenth-century clothing. He floated effortlessly into the room, tipped his plumed hat, and bowed deeply. The grandson was frightened and ran from the room, his grandmother following close behind him. She wished she had remained to see what might have happened but felt it was more important to console her grandson. Of course, by the time she went back to the living room, the apparition was gone.

Six months later, she received a package from the previous owners containing some items they thought she might want. She opened the box to discover a photo of a present-day historic reenactor dressed as one of the Horruytiner governors. He looked just like the man she and her grandson had seen in the living room.

They enjoyed their ghosts and continued to have out-of-the-ordinary experiences. A missing watch was later found in the doorway to the bathroom. Jewelry that had been lost for years turned up in a forgotten box. The washing machine would start running and not stop until a verbal threat was issued. But one of the eeriest things happened in the attic.

The attic area is used strictly for storage and doesn't even have electricity. But lights have been seen shining in the attic space. In addition, the attic once contained an old wooden coffin left by a physician who once lived and practiced in the home. One day the owners heard an unfamiliar noise coming from the attic. They knew there was no one else in the house and chalked it up to their ghosts. The noise persisted and sounded like furniture being scraped across the floor. Curious, they climbed up to the attic and shone a flashlight inside. They saw the dusty wooden casket moving across the floor under its own power.

During the various nightly ghost tours, people continue to see unexplained things at 214 St. George Street, including lights flickering off and on, even in the attic. One weekend, a man reported seeing the figure of a woman through an upstairs window. She was dressed in an old-fashioned long skirt and white shoes, and he could clearly see her going up the stairs. The next moment, a light came on in the bedroom; in a few seconds, it turned off. Not unusual, except that no one had been in the house the entire weekend.

Casa de Horruytiner remains one of the most haunted buildings in St. Augustine, and surely its ghosts will stay, particularly since the home's residents are so amenable to their presence.

The Laughing Men

Now home to the Lightner Museum, the old Hotel Alcazar was built by Henry Flagler and was opened shortly after he opened the splendid Hotel Ponce de Leon just across the street. The Alcazar housed many of the amenities enjoyed by Ponce de Leon patrons, including the largest indoor swimming pool of its day, a bowling alley, a spa, a casino, shops, a ballroom, tennis courts, and more. It was an elegant hotel in its own right and proved a very popular place to stay.

When the ballroom and swimming pool area in the Alcazar underwent renovations, the men doing the construction work related this spooky story. One Friday evening, the construction crew had finished for the day and began packing up their tools. They planned to go out for a beer together, as they often did at the end of the workweek. As they were leaving, one man said he had forgotten something. He told his friends to go ahead and he would catch up with them at the bar.

He went back down to the pool area and heard the distant sound of men laughing. It echoed and reverberated on the concrete surfaces, producing quite an eerie effect. He thought his pals might be playing a trick on him. He quickly strode to the exit. No one was there. He looked out in the parking lot, but all their vehicles were gone.

Frightened, he reluctantly went back in to get his gear and again heard the faint sounds of men talking and laughing. He quickly grabbed his gear and left, vowing not to set foot in there alone again despite the fact that the former patrons of the Hotel Alcazar seem to be having a glorious time.

The de Mesa Sanchez House

According to some people who have worked in the de Mesa Sanchez House at 43 St. George Street, part of the Colonial Spanish Quarter Museum, the place emanates a dark, creepy, ominous feeling that is most strongly felt in the children's room.

One woman who worked there as a guide had a powerful, negative feeling every time she went into the children's room. This undeniable force intrigued her even though she felt it was not altogether kind. Out of curiosity, she decided to photograph

every room in the house for her scrapbook. When the photos were processed, she noticed that the ones taken in the children's room were all marred by the same strange white blur. The other photographs were normal.

Another staff member said that he would prop up a particular sash window using a wooden stick, only to hear the window come crashing down when he turned his back. He would carefully replace the stick, making sure it was secure, and the same thing would happen again. He also reported that furniture moved during the night. He would frequently open up in the morning, only to find that the dust on the floor indicated that furniture had been dragged several inches across the floor.

This widely visited house has generated a lot of interest from paranormal investigators. A family of psychics toured the house and described it as being surrounded by a "bubble of evil." The psychic information they claim to have received about the death of a young girl who had lived in the house was very different from the story on record. History tells us that she drowned accidentally, but they felt that she was murdered and that her killer went unpunished.

A Tale of Two Sisters

In the section of town called North City, two spinster sisters rented an apartment. They had lived together most of their long lives and, surprisingly, had never encountered one moment of discord.

That all changed, however. Weird things began to happen. They would arrive home to find that items such as books, lamps, and vases had been moved from one location to another. Some mornings they would come down to the kitchen to find the dining table strewn with crumbs. Each sister suspected the other, but neither wanted to make waves or accusations, so it was never talked about. It wasn't until they came home together one night and heard noises coming from inside the apartment that they realized it was more than they had originally believed.

One of the sisters was so afraid that she decided she could no longer live in the apartment. The other sister didn't want to admit defeat—or fear, for that matter—and decided to stay. She convinced herself that it was only her imagination or that it really had been her sister moving things around and leaving crumbs on the table. They were becoming a bit forgetful, she had to admit. And besides, now that her sister was gone, she might have some peace and quiet.

Then one night a remarkably strange thing happened. In the early hours of the morning, the woman was abruptly awakened from a deep sleep by a loud rattling noise. She didn't recognize the sound at first but realized it was the front door opening. She was too afraid to get out of bed. Then she saw the knob of her bedroom door turning. The next moment the bedroom door opened and closed on its own, and all she could see was a disembodied hand on the handle.

Petrified, she opened her mouth to scream, but no sound came out. She stayed put for a few moments and then forced herself to get up to see if anyone was there. She called out and looked around, but there wasn't another soul in the apartment.

A Hanging in the Plaza

In the latter part of the seventeenth century, pirates cruised along the coast of Florida in search of ships to prey upon. Spanish treasure fleets sailed from Central and South America back to Spain, laden with gold, silver, and gemstones and making use of the Gulf Stream, sailing right past St. Augustine. Spanish soldiers were stationed on Anastasia Island to protect their treasure ships and the city.

One day Spanish soldiers encountered eleven Englishmen who had been shipwrecked on Anastasia Island. Immediately arrested and questioned, they claimed they were only looking for food and begged for mercy. Not surprisingly, the Spanish were reluctant to believe them. The men were taken to St. Augustine, where they were forced to admit to being pirates.

In most cases, the punishment for piracy was death, and the favored method was unusually primitive and cruel—the garrote. Originally a sliding metal collar with a rope around it, it was placed around the victim's neck and tightened until he could no longer breathe. In St. Augustine, only a rope was used. A tall pole was anchored securely in the ground or to a platform. The pole had a hole through it at about shoulder height. A rope was passed through the hole and placed around the victim's neck. Attached to the other end of the rope was a long wooden stick, which the executioner would smartly twist until the victim strangled to death.

The Spanish discovered that the leader of the Englishmen was named Andrew Ransom. As the leader of the group, he was sentenced to death. The other ten men lucked out: They received extended prison sentences.

Executions were public affairs, and the entire town turned out to watch. A platform was erected on the west side of the plaza, the garrote pole and rope in place. Ransom was paraded from the Castillo, where he had been imprisoned, to the plaza. Citizens eagerly lined the street to watch him being led to his gruesome death.

At the plaza, Ransom was guided up to the scaffold, and the rope was wrapped securely around his neck. Andrew Ransom would die without the dignity of a hood. The excited and overheated crowd pressed closer to get a better look as Alonso Solana read out the court's verdict. With the roll of a drum, the executioner began twisting the rope, one sharp turn at a time.

At that moment, Ransom reached into his pocket, drew out his rosary, and began to pray fervently. The parish priest rushed to the front of the crowd. Why would an Englishman, presumably a Protestant, say the rosary?

Five times the rope turned tighter and tighter, bringing Ransom closer to death. But on the sixth turn, the rope snapped and Ransom slumped to the ground, red in the face and gasping for breath. The priest pushed forward, proclaiming this was an act of God, a miracle. He helped Ransom back to the church, where the saved man lived under its protection.

Ever grateful to the priest, Ransom became a devout Catholic. He worked hard. He paid his debt to society and service to the crown working as a stonemason on the Castillo de San

Marcos. Everyone considered him a clever and blessed man. After twelve years of backbreaking labor, he finally redeemed himself in the eyes of the law. Ransom was a free man who had survived, astonishingly, by a simple "twist of fate."

Room 3-A

Situated at 279 St. George Street is the beautiful St. Francis Inn. Built of coquina in 1791 during the Second Spanish Period, it's a great example of Old World architecture combined with New World elegance.

In the mid-nineteenth century, a military officer and his family moved into the house. They opened their home to their nephew, a young man on the verge of adulthood. He was extremely grateful to be living with them in their spacious St. Augustine home.

The household employed a pretty, young servant, and it wasn't long before she and the nephew fell desperately in love. Knowing their relationship would not be approved of, they would sneak up to the attic to have time alone. One afternoon, the uncle discovered their secret meeting place. Outraged, he sent the servant girl away and told his nephew he must never

see her again. Depressed and despondent, the nephew hanged himself in the attic, which is now room 3-A.

It is believed that the ghost of the young servant girl has returned to the St. Francis Inn. Employees as well as guests have seen her walking up the stairs to room 3-A. She is always dressed in white, and those who first saw her began to call her Lily.

One of the inn's housekeeping staff members would turn the TV on in room 3-A while she cleaned to keep her company. She joked, "Lily doesn't like MTV," because when she left the room for a moment to get fresh linens or towels, upon her return the TV would be off.

A woman staying alone in room 3-A was startled awake by a loud thud. She got up and found the entire contents of her purse strewn across the floor. There was no reason that the purse would have fallen from the dresser by itself, let alone the contents scatter across the floor the way they did. Another woman woke to find her luggage-style cosmetics case full of water, everything inside soaked.

The oddest story of all is about a man who woke up *under*

the bed. He claims he has no idea how he got there and hadn't had one drop to drink that night. He was wedged so far under the bed that he couldn't extricate himself and had to call for help to get out. His wails were finally answered by a staff member, who kindly helped him escape. Nothing was injured except his pride.

It also seems that Lily's passion is still ignited from time to time. A newlywed couple once stayed in room 3-A. In the early morning hours, the husband was awakened by a passionate kiss. Assuming it was his wife, he was quite surprised when he turned over to find her sound asleep.

Not all of the paranormal events at the St. Francis Inn are confined to room 3-A. A couple visiting for the weekend spent their last night in town having an early dinner. They enjoyed a leisurely walk back to the inn, went up to their room, relaxed a bit, and then got ready for bed. The wife was very tired and fell asleep almost immediately. The husband tossed and turned and couldn't fall asleep. He was about to get up and read for a while when a bizarre sensation came over him. He described it as someone "trying to enter my consciousness." He said it was neither a good nor a bad feeling, but it did concern and frighten him, so he got up and went outside for some fresh air and a short walk.

He returned to the room about fifteen minutes later and lay back down on the bed, but the same invasive and persistent feeling took over. He didn't want to upset his wife, so he didn't wake her. This time he allowed the feeling to envelop his consciousness. He wondered if he was having an out-of-body experience. Time seemed to stand still and it felt as if a long time had passed, but when he shook the feeling off and looked at the clock, only a few minutes had actually passed. He left the room again, this time for a cup of coffee. When he returned, the presence was gone. He finally relaxed and drifted off into a deep slumber.

White Hair
and a Beard

South of the plaza, a family owned a house they had inherited from their aunt, a woman who even in death proved surprising. When they took possession of the house, they sorted through the aunt's personal effects and faced quite a bit of cleaning.

One afternoon the mother and daughter started to tackle the job. They sorted through a lot of boxes and found mostly rubbish. However, they were surprised to find in one large box a number of things that had to do with the occult: Ouija boards, magazines about black magic, and other strange objects. They had no idea that their aunt was even remotely interested in such things. Not wanting to keep any of the things they had found, they put all of the items on the curb for the trash collector.

The next day the daughter went to the house to do more cleaning. She was tidying up downstairs when she heard a faint thumping noise coming from above. She thought it might be a squirrel or other small animal in the attic. She ignored it and continued working. The noise became louder and more persistent, however, and she ran from the house to tell her family what she had heard. Her parents were sure it must have been a raccoon, squirrel, or some other animal. Once she calmed down, she decided they were more than likely right.

Mother and daughter returned in a couple of days to finish up, and again the sounds began. The mother called her husband, who came immediately. He searched the house thoroughly but didn't find anything that could have caused the noise. There was no explanation whatsoever for the strange thumping sounds.

In light of discovering their departed aunt's hidden hobbies, the noise worried the family. They asked a psychic friend to come to the house. Immediately upon entering the home, she felt the presence of a spirit that had recently arrived, a man with white hair and a white beard. The mother remembered seeing a photo of a man with white hair and a white beard among the aunt's belongings. When she showed the psychic the photo, the medium said, "Yes, this is the man." The photo was a picture of a boyfriend the aunt once had. Though the family had not known him well, none of them had cared for him.

After a while, they left the house, shutting off all the lights on their way out. On the way home, they realized they had forgotten their extra set of keys and went back to get them. They were shocked to find every single light in the house blazing and all the doors still locked.

The St. Augustine Lighthouse

Lighthouses the world over have ghosts associated with them, and the St. Augustine Lighthouse is no exception.

The magnificent brick tower, with its striking black-and-white spiral design and bright red top, rises 165 feet above sea level. Completed in 1874, the tower still houses a working light. The lighthouse complex, located at 81 Lighthouse Avenue on Anastasia Island, also contains a beautifully restored lightkeeper's house, which is now home to the St. Augustine Lighthouse Museum.

The St. Augustine Lighthouse has been the subject of numerous paranormal investigations and television reports. It is considered by many people to be the most haunted lighthouse in America. Numerous pictures, videos, and audio recordings claiming to capture paranormal activity in the tower and lightkeeper's house can be found online. The *Ghost Hunters* television crew recorded some amazing audio, including the sound of

a woman crying out, "Help me. . . . Help me." They also captured some startling images inside the tower.

One of the most widely seen spirits is a man who roams the basement of the lightkeeper's house. Visitors often smell cigar smoke when no one around them is smoking. This may be the ghost of one of the former lightkeepers.

No doubt the saddest story connected to the lighthouse is that of Hezekiah Pittee, who was the superintendent when the lighthouse was being built. When it became evident that the job would be ongoing, Pittee moved his wife and five children from Maine so they could live onsite during construction. It was a fabulous place for his children; they could play outside year-round and there was a lot of open space with the Salt Run close by. The children had the run of the area and enjoyed playing in a small rail car that was on the property. Used to carry supplies up to the lighthouse, the rail car ran on tracks that led from the lighthouse down toward the pier that went out into the Salt Run. It must have been great fun for the children to jump into the cart and push it up and down the tracks.

One day it all went horribly wrong. Five children were playing in the cart when it went out of control and careered off the pier and into the water. Some of the construction workers ran down as fast as they could. Two of the children were saved but three drowned, including two of Pittee's daughters, Mary, aged 15, and Eliza, 13. The other dead girl might have been the daughter of one of the workers. No one knew what caused the cart to crash into the water, but the tragic event devastated the families involved and the entire community.

Visitors to the lighthouse have heard the echoes of young girls laughing, both on the grounds and inside the lighthouse. People have also seen the figure of a young girl wearing a dark blue dress and a large bow in her hair—exactly the way Mary was dressed the day she drowned.

About the Authors

Suzy Cain frittered away her youth in Turkey, Brazil, and Florida. She holds a Master of Fine Arts degree from Florida Atlantic University and a Bachelor of Fine Arts degree from the University of Florida. She's tried out various careers, from making strippers' costumes to social work to ghost tour guide in St. Augustine, where she learned these wonderful stories. Suzy and her family moved to Wellington, New Zealand, in 2006. She currently works for the biennial, multi-arts New Zealand Festival.

Dianne Jacoby, a fourth-generation Floridian living in St. Augustine, is an actress and historical dramatist. She has written and performs in a number of one-woman dramas, including her well-known *The Three Mrs. Flaglers,* which she performs for private groups, libraries, and historical societies. Previously an adjunct professor of art at Flagler College, Dianne now coordinates Stetson University's Elderhostel/Road Scholar programs in St. Augustine.

Dianne has exhibited her drawings and paintings throughout the United States and has also illustrated a number of books.

Here are some other books from Pineapple Press on related topics. For a complete catalog, write to Pineapple Press, P.O. Box 3889, Sarasota, Florida 34230-3889, or call (800) 746-3275. Or visit our website at www.pineapplepress.com.

Ghosts of St. Augustine by Dave Lapham. The unique and often turbulent history of America's oldest city is told in twenty-four spooky stories that cover four hundred years' worth of ghosts.

Ancient City Hauntings by Dave Lapham. In this sequel to *Ghosts of St. Augustine,* the author takes you on more quests for supernatural experiences through the dark, enduring streets of the Ancient City. Come visit the Oldest House, the Old Jail, Ripley's, all the many haunted B&Bs, and more.

Oldest Ghosts by Karen Harvey. In St. Augustine, ghostly apparitions are as intriguing as the city's history.

Florida's Ghostly Legends and Haunted Folklore, Volume 1: *South and Central Florida; Florida's Ghostly Legends and Haunted Folklore,* Volume 2: *North Florida and St. Augustine;* and *Florida's Ghostly Legends and Haunted Folklore,* Volume 3: *The Gulf Coast and Pensacola* by Greg Jenkins. The history and legends behind a number of Florida's haunted locations, plus bone-chilling accounts taken from firsthand witnesses of spooky phenomena. Volume 1 locations include Key West's La Concha Hotel, the Everglades, Stetson University, and the Sunshine

Skyway Bridge. Volume 2 includes Silver Springs National Park, Flagler College, and the St. Augustine Lighthouse. Volume 3 covers the historic city of Pensacola and continues southward through the Tampa area, Sarasota, and Naples.

Chronicles of the Strange and Uncanny in Florida by Greg Jenkins. Open these files to explore Florida's darker avenues for evidence of the extraordinary and the fantastic. Encounter the Skunk Ape, El Cupacabra, a phantom clown, and some bloodthirsty vampires.

Haunted Lighthouses and How to Find Them by George Steitz. A grand tour of the legends of these bewitched and bewitching monuments. Meet a cast of intriguing characters, including noted historians, people who work in lighthouses, and the ghosts themselves.

The Reaper of St. George Street by Andre Frattino. In this first graphic novel published by Pineapple Press, Andre Frattino has created unforgettable characters and a spooky story that centers on an evil spirit. Arriving in haunted St. Augustine to attend college, skeptic Will is soon thrust into a mystery he wants no part of. But the girl he's falling in love with needs his help to rid her of the nightmares plaguing her sleep. Aided by a motley crew of ghost hunters—a pickpocket, a modern-day witch, a retired pirate, and a comic book nerd—Will must discover why a murderous poltergeist named the Reaper of St. George Street is wreaking havoc.

Lost Souls of Savannah by Andre Frattino. In the sequel to *The Reaper of St. George Street,* we follow the spirit Victor, who has spent more of his "life" dead than alive. Just as purgatory becomes too much for him, he learns of a hoodoo priestess in Georgia who could give him life again, but at a price. Before she can grant his wish, he must collect the five most infamous souls of Savannah. It won't be an easy job, but along the way Victor will make new friends—and new enemies—and for the first time in a long time, he will feel alive . . . almost.

Florida Ghost Stories by Robert R. Jones. Stories of ghosts and tall tales of strange happenings will give you goose bumps and make your hair stand on end.

Haunting Sunshine by Jack Powell. Take a wild ride through the shadows of the Sunshine State in this collection of deliciously creepy stories of ghosts in the theaters, churches, and historic places of Florida.

The Ghost Orchid Ghost and Other Tales from the Swamp by Doug Alderson. Florida's famous swamps—from the Everglades to Mosquito Lagoon to Tate's Hell—serve as fitting backdrops for these chilling original stories. Who but a naturalist can really scare you about what lurks in the swamp? Doug Alderson has been there and *knows*. From the author's notes at the end of each story, you can learn a thing or two about Florida's swamps, creatures, and history, along with storytelling tips.

Haunt Hunter's Guide to Florida by Joyce Elson Moore. Discover the general history and "haunt" history of numerous sites around the state where ghosts reside.

Ghosts of Savannah by Terrance Zepke. Spooky tales of the many ghosts of Savannah, one of America's most haunted cities. Discover why an exorcism had to be performed at the Hampton-Lillibridge House, who haunts the old Candler Hospital, and why a cat haunts the Davenport House. Includes fascinating bits of Savannah history and visiting information.

Best Ghost Tales of North Carolina and *Best Ghost Tales of South Carolina* by Terrance Zepke. From the mountains of North Carolina to South Carolina's Lowcountry, here are more than 50 spooky stories that will keep you up at night.

Ghosts of the Carolina Coasts by Terrance Zepke. Enjoy 32 spine-tingling tales taken from real-life occurrences and Lowcountry lore.

Ghosts and Legends of the Carolina Coasts by Terrance Zepke. This collection of 28 stories ranges from hair-raising tales of horror to fascinating legends culled from Carolina folklore. Learn about the eerie Fire Ship of New Bern, and meet the dreaded Boo Hag.

Ghosts of the Georgia Coast by Don Farrant. Visit crumbling slave cabins, grand mansions and plantation homes, ancient forts, and Indian hideouts to find restless souls, skin-walkers, and protective spirits.

CPSIA information can be obtained at www.ICGtesting.com
Printed in the USA
BVOW09s0208100214

344341BV00005B/9/P